Emmy
the Exaggerating
Elephant

Fenton
the Fearful Frog

Gertie
the Grungy Goat

Herbie
the Happy
Hamster

Ivy
the Impatient
Iguana

Ollie
the Obedient
Ostrich

Perry
the Polite
Porcupine

Queenie
the Quiet Quail

Rupert
the Resourceful
Rhinoceros

Wendy
the Wise
Woodchuck

Xavier
the X-ploring
Xenops

Yori
the Yucky Yak

Ziggy
the Zippy Zebra

NOTE TO PARENTS

<u>Monty See, Monty Do</u>
A story about thinking independently and making choices

In this story, Monty the Mimicking Mouse finds it hard to make his own decisions, and mindlessly imitates everything his AlphaPet friends do and say. When he is about to imitate Nelly's naughty antics, he realizes that he must make up his own mind at last.

In addition to enjoying this funny mystery with your child, you can use it to teach a gentle lesson about the value of making your own decisions about what you'll do and say.

You can also use this story to introduce the letter **M**. As you read about Monty the Mimicking Mouse, ask your child to listen for all the **M** words and point to the objects that begin with **M**. When you've finished reading the story, your child will enjoy doing the activity at the end of the book.

The AlphaPets™ characters were conceived and created by Ruth Lerner Perle.
Characters interpreted and designed by Deborah Colvin Borgo.
Cover/book design and production by Norton & Company.
Logo design by Deborah Colvin Borgo and Nancy S. Norton.
Printed and Manufactured in the United States of America

Monty See,
Monty Do

RUTH LERNER PERLE

Illustrated by Richard Max Kolding

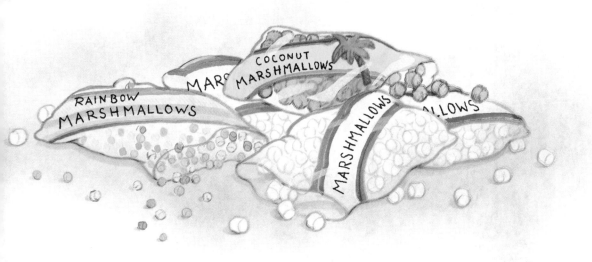

Grolier Enterprises Inc.,   Danbury, Connecticut

One Monday morning in the month of May, Monty the Mimicking Mouse was walking down Maple Street when he met Perry the Polite Porcupine.

"Good morning, Monty," said Perry. "I'm on my way to the market."

"I'll go to the market, too," said Monty.

"What will you buy?" asked Perry.

"I don't know yet," said Monty. "What will *you* buy?"

Perry looked at his long shopping list and said, "I need meat, milk, mustard, macaroni, muffins, maple syrup, and marshmallows."

"That sounds good," said Monty. "I think I'll get meat, milk, mustard, macaroni, muffins, maple syrup, and marshmallows, too."

As Perry and Monty went into the market, they saw the AlphaPets gathered near the door.

"What's going on?" asked Perry.

"What's going on?" asked Monty.

"Haven't you heard?" said Una the Unhappy Unicorn. "A terrible crime has been committed. All the marshmallows have disappeared."

"Someone took them. There isn't a marshmallow to be found!" cried Delilah the Demanding Duck.

"Who would take all the marshmallows?" asked Perry.

"I'll bet an invasion of Martians swooped down and took them," said Sylvester the Stubborn Squirrel.

"Yes, Martians," said Monty.

"I think a band of monsters rode off with them," Delilah said.

"Yes, monsters," Monty agreed.

"Maybe a mad magician made them disappear," said Katy the Kind Koala.

"Yes, a mad magician," Monty repeated.

Justin the Joking Jackal smiled and said, "I know . . . a million mosquitoes each took a tiny bite until the marshmallows were all gone."

"Yes, a million mosquitoes," Monty agreed.

"All this marshmallow talk is making me hungry," said Emmy the Exaggerating Elephant. "Let's go to the Magic Marble Restaurant. We can have a snack and discuss this horrible, awful, disgraceful situation there."

Everyone followed Emmy into the restaurant.

Albert the Absent-minded Alligator was waiting on tables. He gave everyone a paper placemat and a menu. Then he took their orders.

"A slice of pizza with mushrooms, please," said Perry.

"Pizza with mushrooms for me, too," Monty said.

"Extra mozzarella cheese on my slice," Delilah ordered.

"Pizza with extra mozzarella for me, too," Monty said.

"I'll have two slices with meatballs—and plenty of them," Emmy said.

"Two slices with plenty of meatballs for me, too," said Monty.

Sylvester, Katy, and Justin all asked for pepperoni and peppers on their slices of pizza, and so did Monty. Albert finished writing down all the orders and went into the kitchen.

Soon Albert came back carrying a huge tray. He served everyone their pizza slices. Then he put *seven* big slices of pizza on Monty's plate, one on top of the other. What a mish-mash!

"Wow! That's a lot of pizza," said Monty.

"That's what you ordered, Monty. I wrote it down right here on my pad," said Albert. "You ordered what everybody else ordered."

"Ha, ha! Monty see, Monty do!" said Justin.

Monty was too embarrassed to complain, so he ate all the pizza on his plate. By the time he finished, his stomach was so full he could hardly move.

"It's getting late. I'd better go now," Monty said. "Please let me know when the marshmallow mystery is solved."

Monty took some money out of his pocket, paid for his pizza, and went home.

As soon as Monty got home, he brushed his teeth and went straight to bed. But his stomach was so upset that he couldn't sleep. He tossed and he turned and turned and tossed.

At midnight, Monty still could not fall asleep. He got up, filled his hot water bottle, and put it on his tummy.

Then he went and sat down on his window seat and pulled the curtain back. Everything was quiet and dark, except for the full moon shining in the sky.

Monty looked up at the moon. "Why did I order all that pizza?" he said with a great sigh. "I wish I could make up my mind like everyone else. Why can't I ever think for myself? I don't want to be a 'Monty see, Monty do' anymore."

Suddenly Monty saw a light go on in the window next door. It was Nelly the Naughty Newt's house. Through the window Monty could see that Nelly was also awake.

"Hmm," Monty said to himself, "I wonder if Nelly has a tummyache like me. Maybe I can help her feel better."

So Monty put on his moccasins and his coat and went over to Nelly's house.

When Nelly came to the door, she was hiding
something behind her back.

"Hello, Nelly," Monty said. "I saw you from my
window and...."

"Oh, no!" said Nelly. "You didn't see anything."

"But I did," Monty said. "I thought you might not be
feeling well, so I brought you my hot water bottle." When
Nelly opened the door for Monty, she accidentally dropped
the bag of marshmallows she was holding!

"Marshmallows!" Monty cried. "Nelly, are these the
marshmallows from the market?"

"Well...er...yes..." Nelly answered. She picked the
bag up and offered it to Monty. "Help yourself," Nelly
said, taking a marshmallow herself.

Monty was about to take a marshmallow, just like Nelly, but then he put it back.

"These marshmallows don't belong to you. It would be wrong for me to eat them," he said.

"Don't be silly, Monty," said Nelly. "*I'm* eating them, so you can, too."

"I know that I always copy what everyone else does," Monty said, "but this time I won't. You should not have taken those marshmallows, Nelly!"

"I didn't mean any harm," Nelly said. "I know you're right, and now I'm really sorry. What shall I do, Monty?"

Monty thought for awhile. Then he said, "I have an idea! My very own idea. I'll help you put all the marshmallows into a big bag, and you can take them back to the market in the morning."

"Well, okay," Nelly said, "but will you go with me?"

"I will," Monty promised.

Early the next morning, Monty and Nelly brought the marshmallows back to the market.

"Where were they?" Delilah wanted to know.

"I took them, and I'm sorry," Nelly said. She looked at Monty and smiled. "It was Monty who made me realize how wrong I was."

"Well, in a way you helped me too, Nelly," said Monty. "I finally had to think for myself. And you know what? I *like* making up my own mind!"

The AlphaPets cheered, "Good for you, Monty!"

"Hooray!" whooped Emmy. "Let's meet later at the Magic Marble and have a party!"

This time, when Albert came to take the order, Monty thought about what kind of meal *he* really wanted.

"*Mmm, Mmm!*" Monty said, looking at the menu. "I'd like some macaroni and cheese, please, and a malted milkshake. I've had enough pizza for a while."

"What a good idea!" the AlphaPets shouted. "We'll all have the same as Monty!"

Soon the Magic Marble Minstrels started to play.
Everyone clapped their hands and tapped their toes to
the music.

Then the AlphaPets lifted Monty to their shoulders and marched into the street, shouting, "Monty, you are *marvelous!*"

Make up your mind to learn these words
with me.

marshmallows

marbles

muffin

mirror

moon

moccasins

motorcycle

mushroom

menu

Look back at the pictures in this book and try to find these and other things that begin with M.

Aa Bb

Gg Hh

Mm Nn Oo Pp

Uu Vv Ww